Emma and the Food Bank

A CALGARY FOOD BANK BOOK

written by
SUE MCLURE

illustrated by
VAL LAWTON

Emma and the Food Bank
© The Calgary Food Bank, 2014
written by Sue McLure; illustrations by Val Lawton

No part of this publication may be reproduced, stored in a retrieval system or transmitted, in any form or by any means,
without the prior written consent of the author or a licence from The Canadian Copyright Licensing Agency (Access Copyright).
For an Access Copyright licence, visit www.accesscopyright.ca or call toll free to 1-800-893-5777.

Manufactured by Friesens Corporation in Altona, MB, Canada
March 2014
Job #201141

Cataloguing data available from Library and Archives Canada.
ISBN: 978-0-9937113-0-5

Layout and design by Heather Nickel

Printed in Canada

ENVIRONMENTAL BENEFITS STATEMENT

Calgary Food Bank saved the following resources by
printing the pages of this book on chlorine free paper
made with 10% post-consumer waste.

WATER	SOLID WASTE	GREENHOUSE GASES
202	13	37
GALLONS	POUNDS	POUNDS

Environmental impact estimates were made using the Environmental Paper Network
Paper Calculator 3.2. For more information visit www.papercalculator.org.

FSC
www.fsc.org

MIX
Paper from
responsible sources
FSC® C016245

CALGARY
FOOD BANK

Emma loved going grocery shopping with her mom.
They always had fun together.

When Emma's mom asked her to choose a vegetable
for supper, Emma chose her favourite.

"Hey, Mom! Why are you putting other groceries in that box?" asked Emma.

"This is a Food Bank box, Emma," her mom answered.
"Sometimes moms and dads have problems and can't work for some time,
and may need help with groceries. So the Food Bank collects food
from people and gives it to families who need it."

"Mom? Will we need food from the Food Bank one day?"

Emma's mom said, "I hope not, but if our family has problems and we need food,
it's good to know that the Food Bank will help us."

"So, it's not a bank where you save money and get money, right, Mom?
It's a bank that collects food for people who need it."

"That's right, Emma," said her mom.

"Can I give the Food Bank food that I really like?" asked Emma.

"Sure, that's a great idea!" said her mom.

"What else can I do to help the Food Bank?" Emma asked.

"Well, when you're 12 years old, you can go to the Food Bank with Granddad to help sort groceries and put together food hampers, just like your cousins do when they have a day off school," Emma's mom answered.

"But I'm not going to be 12 for a long time!" said Emma.
"How can I help now?"

"How about we put together a birthday bag?
Let's gather things like candles, a cake mix,
balloons and a small toy,"
Emma's mom suggested.

"Like my Cinnamon Bear?" asked Emma.

"Yes!" said Emma's mom.
"Then the Food Bank will make sure
a family with a birthday boy or girl
gets it in their hamper."

"There's something else you can do," said Emma's mom.

"What?" asked Emma.

"You're having your birthday party soon. You can ask your guests to bring a food item, like a jar of peanut butter or a box of pasta...

...then, after the party, you and I can take the food to the Food Bank. They will weigh it, tell us how much we collected, and how many people you helped!" said Emma's mom.

"And I can take the birthday bag we made so another girl or boy can have a party too!" Emma shouted.

"I like a bank that gives people food AND birthday presents!"